The Monster House

KELLY
PUBLISHING

Sally Rogers
Illustrated by Úna Woods

Illustrated by Úna Woods. Published in Ireland by Orla Kelly Publishing.

Dedication

To Harry and Hollie. My inspiration, my fuel and my fire.

I went to visit the monster house,

The one on top of the hill.

It truly was lots of fun,

No! Really! What a thrill.

The door slowly opened,

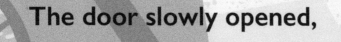

Creek! Snap! Crack!

Behind the door was a shadowy figure,

Wait! That's just my friend Jack.

"Come in." he boomed in his thundery voice.

He looked like a Frankenstein,

With bolts each side of his neck,

Glistening as the moon shined.

He has ears that screw on,

And a switch for a nose.

You won't believe what else he has.

That's right! Batteries for toes.

His skin is green with scars all around,

He has really long arms, almost touching the ground.

But he is my friend so it dosen't matter.

"This way" he said as he picked up a platter.

The platter had snacks of maggots and eyes.

One Mouse, three spiders and about seven flies.

We walked into the dining room and just like that,

The mouse escaped the platter and was chased by the cat.

And sitting in the corner over there in a chair,

Was a charming looking Werewolf combing his hair.

"OH! Nice to meet you." He jumped up and said.

"Don't worry" he laughed, as he patted my head.

"I can't help but wonder why you look so suspicious."

He laughed once again. "You do smell delicious."

In the corner was a Ghost who was practising her scare.

"Wow! That is spooky!" I said with care.

"Whhhyyyy……thhaaankk…..yyoooouuuu…." she returned

beaming with pride.

And off she floated with a smile extra wide.

At the fireplace was a Vampire, sharpening his teeth.

"Hello." He said "My name is Keith."

He took my hand and gave it a shake,

But he was so strong my hand had an ache.

The mouse zoomed past being chased by the cat,

Jack said "Aww.... look, they're having a spat!"

We laughed and we joked then Jack and I moved on.

In the kitchen we met a witch singing a song.

"Body part soup,

In the cauldron today,

Body part soup,

Hiphip! HOORAY!"

"What a wonderful song" I told her with glee.

"Thank you, dear Bobby." She smiled back at me.

At the table sat a Mummy knitting more bandages.

Getting ready for wrapping, I wonder how he manages?

There was a zombie in the fridge, chewing on her own arm.

"Don't worry about me," she said as I stared.

"It will do me no harm."

I smiled once again and carried on through.

I wondered where we were going, if only I knew.

At the end of the hallway, there was another old door.

"At Last." Boomed Jack, "Door number four."

We went on in and flicked on the light.

"SURPRISE!"

Oh my! What a wonderful sight.

It was a monster birthday party for me in the end.

"Happy Birthday dear Bobby, you are a true friend."

All my monster friends gathered round just for me.

I wondered how this all came to be.

My trip to the monster house on the top of the hill,

Well it truly was the most magnificent, extraordinary thrill.

Acknowledgements

Without so many people, this story would not have come to life.

Thank you to my partner Nicholas, for encouraging me to keep going and not give up and for so much more. Your love and support has kept my head clear and my feet grounded.

When I sat down to write this story, Harry, you were so excited. Your involvement has made this an incredibly special story for me. Of all the pieces I have written, you have made this one, my favourite. You and your sister are always an inspiration. Hollie, your joy and devilment bring light to my life even on the darkest of days. Stay determined.

To Úna Woods thank you for all your hard work. Your illustrations have brought so much life to my story. You were an absolute pleasure to work with and without your fantastic artwork The Monster House would still just be scraps of paper in an old notebook.

Thank you to Orla Kelly for helping me with my self-publishing journey. Without you, this book wouldn't be available to anyone. Technology and I do not mix very well, your help, and support is truly appreciated.

About the Author

Sally Rogers is the mother of two perfectly tornado like children. Living in a small town and raising her two children with her partner has given her the time to revisit a long term past time of writing. From a young age Sally has been writing stories, but as time moved on and adult life took over, the notebooks closed, and the dust settled. Having children made her revisit those dusty old notebooks, wanting to write fun stories for her children. The Monster House is the debut book for Sally, written alongside her children on Halloween night. Her son is the reason Jack has some of his interesting features.

Dear Reader,

If you enjoyed this book, would you kindly post a short review on Amazon or Goodreads? Your feedback will make all the difference to getting the word out about this book.
To leave a review on Amazon, type in the book title. When you have found it, go to the book page.Please scroll to the bottom of the page to where it says 'Write a Review' and then submit your review.
Thank you in advance.

If you would like a complimentary gift of a poster to download, please email me on SallyAnne. Stories@gmail.com and I will email it back to you.

Best wishes

Sally

Lightning Source UK Ltd.
Milton Keynes UK
UKHW050901140721
387106UK00005B/78